FATHER SKY, MOTHER EARTH AND ME

FATHER SKY, MOTHER EARTH AND ME

SEANA COUGHLIN

Author Reputation Press LLC
45 Dan Road Suite 36
Canton MA 02021
www.authorreputationpress.com
Hotline: 1(800) 220-7660
Fax: 1(855) 752-6001

Ordering Information:
Quantity Sales. Special discounts are available on quantity purchases by corporations, associations, and others. For details, contact the publisher at the address above.

Printed in the United States of America.

ISBN-13	Softcover	978-1-64961-568-8
	eBook	978-1-64961-569-5
	Hardback	978-1-64961-590-9

Library of Congress Control Number: 2021911995

This book is dedicated to my son
Skyler, always my Angel on
Earth and now in Heaven.
I love and miss you endlessly.

Mom

Hello friend!
Hello friend!

"Hello friend," The sun said to Sky.

"Hello friend," Sky said to the sun.

"I will work together with you when I shine down on you and every living thing on Earth. My sunshine makes leaves in the trees and plants turn green and grow healthy. I am the source of all energy, heat and light. Animals lay in my warm rays to raise their body temperature and be active. Humans, animals and plants on Earth need the sun because it gives us energy. Your body needs vitamin D to grow strong bones and connect you to the stars."

"Yep. We do work together. Thank you, bright and warm sun." Sky said with a comforted feeling inside his heart.

Hi friend!
Hi friend!

"Hi friend," said the cardinal, hummingbird, hawk, owl, deer and butterfly .

"Hi friend," said Sky.

"We will help you receive a message from your loved ones and Angels in Heaven. HELLO! I LOVE YOU! I AM ALWAYS BY YOUR SIDE! Are the words we are sending to you when you see us close to you in nature. You watch us quietly fly by or sit on a tree branch outside of your window, and your mind and spirit hear our words of love."

"Yep. We do help each other. Thank you Spirit animals." Sky said with a comforted feeling inside his soul.

Hi friend!
Hi friend!

"Hi friend," The rainbow said to Sky.

"Hi friend," Sky said to the rainbow.

"I will help you build a bridge to the Heavenly realms above you. I will help your loved ones on their journey to Heaven. I will help YOU remember your Spirit - the light inside of you that shines so bright, but you can't touch it...... just like me. You can never touch a rainbow, but you can see my beautiful colors light up the sky and you know I am real."

"Yep. We do help each other. Thank you rainbow." Sky said with a safe feeling inside his heart.

Hello friend!
Hello friend!
KR3W

"Hello friend," The little boy's voice inside spoke to him.

"Hello friend," Sky said to his positive and loving voice inside.

"I will take care of you by making safe and healthy choices with you. Listen to my gentle words and let them help you be your best.

Ask for what you need and then feel inside your heart and mind and.... LISTEN. My answer will ALWAYS come to you. It is often the first thought that comes into your mind. I might sound like you, or a special loved one in Heaven or an Angel so kind and caring. I will never be mean or be a bully, and if I try to trick you, tell me you will wait to listen for my friendly voice to come back. Your loving, guiding voice is the only true voice inside of you."

"Yep. We do take care of each other.

Thank you, inside voice." Sky said with a comforted feeling inside his soul.

Hi friend!
Hi friend!

"Hi friend," The water said to Sky.

"Hi friend," Sky said to the water.

"We work together because water covers MOST of the Earth's surface and water is MOST of your human body. I will help you and every living thing by giving you fresh water to drink. Drink from my rivers and fill your body with me. Help my waters stay clean so I am available for ALL beings, plants and animals, forever."

"Yep. We do work together. Thank you, water." Sky said with a comforted feeling inside his heart.

Hi friend!
Hi friend!

"Hi friend," The dark night sky and bright, sparkly stars said to Sky.

"Hi friend," Sky said to the night sky and bright stars.

"We work together by quieting the earth in a blanket of sparkly darkness so that all living things can sleep and recharge for a new day. So that all living things can make way for dream time. When your body sleeps, your mind dreams. These dreams connect to your Angels in the Heavenly realms and you receive messages of love and gentle guidance for the new day."

"Do you know that the bones in your body are made with a little bit of stardust in them? We have this in common. We are connected by all that we are made of. Maybe this is why you shine bright just like I do."

"Yep. We do work together. Thank you, night sky and sparkly stars." Sky said with a comforted feeling inside his soul.

Hello friend!
Hello friend!

"Hello friend," The bright full moon said to Sky "Hello friend," Sky said to the moon.

"We help each other by you watching me grow bigger or smaller each night. We are connected through the molecules in the blood that runs through the veins in your body. I may affect how you feel. When I am full and round and bright, you may feel a lot of energy. When I am small and crescent shaped, you may feel less energy. Let me guide your day.

When you were born, you were given a moon sign.

What is your moon sign? What is the moon's description of you?"

"Yep. We do help each other. Thank you, full moon." Sky said with a comforted feeling inside his heart

KR3W

"We help each other. We work together and we take care of each other. That's what friends do."

Father Sky, Mother Earth and Me

CPSIA information can be obtained
at www.ICGtesting.com
Printed in the USA
LVHW070307160322
713570LV00002B/99

* 9 7 8 1 6 4 9 6 1 5 6 8 8 *